I LOVE YOU, MOMMY!

BY EDIE EVANS
ILLUSTRATED BY RUSTY FLETCHER

For my Mom, Florence Levin

—E.E.

A GOLDEN BOOK • NEW YORK

Copyright © 1999 by Random House, Inc. All rights reserved. Published in the United States by Golden Books, an imprint of Random House Children's Books, a division of Random House, Inc., New York. GOLDEN BOOKS, A GOLDEN BOOK, A LITTLE GOLDEN BOOK, the G colophon, and the distinctive gold spine are registered trademarks of Random House, Inc.
www.goldenbooks.com
www.randomhouse.com/kids
Educators and librarians, for a variety of teaching tools, visit us at www.randomhouse.com/teachers
Library of Congress Control Number: 99-067606
ISBN: 978-0-307-99507-0
Printed in the United States of America
30 29

My Mommy always finds a way
to make me feel special every day.
Because she's fun and caring, too,
I love everything we do.

We sometimes go to the street fair
to see the neat attractions there.
Maybe we'll eat hot dogs on sticks
and see a magician doing tricks.

At the stadium we clap and cheer
for the baseball players every year.
Together we love to stand and shout,
"One! Two! Three strikes—you're out!"

When lightning comes and raindrops fall,
we stay indoors and have a ball.
We bake bread, then eat it warm,
and forget about the thunderstorm.

The museum I like best of all
is filled with dinosaurs big and tall.
Mommy takes me all around
to see the bones found in the ground.

Quiet time inside is nice.
We play a game—sometimes twice—
or make puppets from old socks
Mommy keeps in a homemade box.

Basketball is my favorite sport.
I shoot and dribble down the court.
Mom's the coach and she helps me
to be the best that I can be.

Everything we do and see
becomes a treasured memory.
I love you, Mommy, and this is true:
The greatest gift is a hug from you!